< DOING TIME ONLINE >

< DOING TIME ONLINE >

JAN SIEBOLD

Albert Whitman and Company

Morton Grove, Illinois

Library of Congress Cataloging-in-Publication Data

Siebold, Jan.

Doing time online / Jan Siebold.

p. cm.

Summary: After he is involved in a prank that led to an elderly woman's
injury, twelve-year-old Mitchell must make amends by participating in a
police program in which he chats online with a nursing home resident.

ISBN 0-8075-5959-8 (hardcover) ISBN 0-8075-1665-1 (paperback)

[1. Old age — Fiction. 2. Nursing homes — Fiction. 3. Punishment — Fiction.]

I. Title. PZ7.S5665 Do 2002 [Fic] — dc21 2001004092

Text © copyright 2002 by Jan Siebold.

Cover illustration © copyright 2002 by Layne Johnson.

Published in 2002 by Albert Whitman & Company,

6340 Oakton Street, Morton Grove, Illinois 60053-2723.

Published simultaneously in Canada by Fitzhenry & Whiteside, Markham, Ontario.

Printed in the United States of America.

12 11 10 9 8 7 6 5 4 3

The design is by Scott Piehl.

For my parents and grandparents,
and for the Wooties of the world.

Officer MacDougal led me down the hallway of the Franklin Police Department and into a small room. He motioned to a chair which was placed in front of a computer terminal.

"Have a seat, Mitchell," he said. "The computer is all ready to go. Your ID code is 'Mitch.' The nursing home ID is 'MapleG.' Just type your message, and the folks at Maple Grove will know you're starting. I'll be back at four o'clock to let you out. No rudeness or foul language, understand?"

I nodded. A practical joke backfires, and suddenly you're treated like Jack the Ripper. I didn't mean it, I wanted to shout. If I could take back that night, I'd do it in a second. It wasn't even my fault, but I took the fall. Now I was stuck coming here — *the police station* — two afternoons a week.

Officer MacDougal closed the door behind him. I stared at the blinking cursor on the screen. Whose idea was this, anyway?

Probably some social worker type of person had come up with this program called "O.L.D. Friend" for juvenile offenders. The O.L.D. stands for "Online Discussion." I suppose you could also take it to mean "old" as in "longtime," or "old" as in "ancient." I wasn't interested in either one. Basically, I had to show up at the police station every Tuesday and Thursday for a month to have a computer "chat" with a resident of the Maple Grove Nursing Home somewhere across the state.

I guess the logic behind the whole plan was that old people have a lot of wisdom to share. It's not that I have anything against senior citizens. In fact, I hope to be one myself someday. I just wasn't sure that I could "chat" with one for an entire half-hour. I didn't have anything to say to this person, and I certainly didn't need to sit and read some lecture about the good old days when kids had to walk eight miles to school in all kinds of weather.

I looked around the tiny room. The walls were painted schoolroom green. A poster on the wall advertised a car wash to benefit the local Students Against Drunk Drivers chapter.

The computer sat on a wooden table. I could see a sticky ring about the size of a soda can on the tabletop. No one had offered me anything to drink. Near the ring, someone had carved the word "Rats" in jagged letters.

Glancing at my watch, I saw that it was almost three-forty-five. I had taken keyboarding in school the year before, and had gotten much better at it. I took a deep breath and began to type.

Mitch: Hi. My name is Mitchell Riley. What's your name?

A few seconds went by, and then words began to slowly appear below mine on the screen.

MapleG: I'm Wootie Hayes. You're late.

Mitch: Sorry. It took longer than I thought to walk here from school.

MapleG: Then I guess you'll have to walk faster next time.

It was hard to tell whether or not this person was kidding. I typed:

Mitch: I guess so.

A minute or so went by. There was no answer, so I wrote:

Mitch: Are you a man or a woman? I've never heard the name Wootie.

MapleG: I used to be a woman. Now I'm a shriveled-up old lady. When I was born, my sister was only three years old. Apparently she couldn't pronounce my real name, Ruthie. It kept coming out "Wootie." My parents started calling me that and it stuck. Meanwhile, my sister had a beautiful name — Rose. It never seemed fair to me that she stuck me with such a horrible name and went through life with such a pretty one herself.

Mitch: I bet people don't have any trouble remembering the name Wootie.

MapleG: That's for sure. My husband Lou always said that I'm one of a kind, just like my name. I've actually come to like it. Do you have any brothers or sisters?

Mitch: No. It's just me and my dad. My mom died when I was a little kid.

MapleG: How old are you?

Mitch: Twelve. How about you?

MapleG: I'm NOT twelve.

I paused, and typed:

Mitch: How do you like it at Maple Grove?

MapleG: Ha! That's a good one. I'll bet there's not a single maple tree, much less a whole grove of them, within a mile of this miserable place.

Mitch: What's wrong with it?

MapleG: There's no privacy. The food is bland. The head nurse on my floor is a pain. Her name is Mrs. Nagle, but I call her Nurse Nag-a-lot. Mostly, I'm bored out of my skull. I'm not used to just sitting around. My roommate is nice enough, but she's the BINGO queen of the world. She's always trying to drag me to the rec room for the daily game. Last week she won a prize. Know what it was? Some of those little tissues that you carry in your purse. You would have thought it was a million dollars, the way she carried on.

I could tell that old Wootie was on a roll now.

Mitch: How long have you been there?

MapleG: Oh, about three months, I guess. Too long, that's for sure.

Mitch: Where did you live before?

MapleG: I STILL live in Colesville. My house is there. Lou laid the bricks for it himself. That's what he did for a living. We moved in right after we got married. I did the bookkeeping for him. Lou worked right up until the day he died. It doesn't seem possible that he's been gone for almost three years. I can't wait to leave this place and go home. There's a beautiful REAL maple tree there right outside my kitchen window.

Mitch: Why are you at Maple Grove?

MapleG: Back in June, I fell and broke my hip. It was a dumb accident. I was hanging out the wash and tripped over the clothes basket. I lay there for two hours until the paper boy came along and rescued me. I ended up having surgery on my hip, but it's still giving me trouble. The physical therapy doesn't seem to be helping. Why are YOU there?

Mitch: You mean at the police station?

MapleG: Of course that's what I mean.

I had to stop for a moment.

Mitch: Mine was an accident, too. It was supposed to be a joke, but it backfired and someone got hurt.

Just then, Officer MacDougal opened the door and stuck his head into the room.

"Five more minutes, Mitchell," he said.

I nodded and turned back to the keyboard. I couldn't believe that it was already almost four o'clock. I guess typing a conversation takes a lot longer than talking face to face. I wrote:

Mitch: I have to go now.

MapleG: That's okay. Wallace is here anyway.

Mitch: Who's Wallace?

MapleG: He's the nice young man who delivers me from place to place around here. I guess you could call him my wheelchair chauffeur. Will you be back Thursday?

Mitch: Yes.

MapleG: Be on time.

Mitch: I'll try.

I stared at the screen, expecting a final message, but none came. Officer MacDougal led me back out, and we left.

<< 4:05 P.M. >>

The deal was that Officer MacDougal would give me a ride home. He dropped me off at the corner of my street.

As I walked the rest of the way, I thought about Wootie Hayes. Her messages had surprised me. I guess I had expected them to be sweet and sugary and packed with grand-motherly advice. Old Wootie was definitely a straight shooter.

As I started to walk up the driveway, a voice from behind interrupted my thoughts.

"Hey. It's Really Riley."

I didn't have to turn around to know whose voice it was. Randall "Trotter" Trotman caught up with me and started to walk along.

When Trotter moved into the neighborhood last year, I went over to introduce myself. After hearing my last name, he asked, "Really? Riley? Is it really Riley? Really?"

It may have seemed clever at the time, but after about the billionth time, it had grown old.

"Hey, Trotter," I said, and kept walking.

"So how's my old buddy doing?" he asked, punching me on the arm.

I shrugged and answered, "Okay."

"You're late coming home from school today," said Trotter. He was carrying an open package of chocolate-chip cookies. Crumbs dotted his chin and the front of his shirt. Melted chocolate lined the corners of his mouth.

I wouldn't have accepted a cookie from Trotter, but I didn't have to worry. He didn't offer me one. Trotter could be in a room full of

starving children and he wouldn't offer one.
He's not known for being a humanitarian.

"I had to go someplace after school," I told
him.

"Oh, that's right," he said. "Today's the day
you started doing time at the police station. Too
bad about that. I've been home practicing my
lay-up shot."

Trotter grinned. I looked at him. He was a
good six inches taller than me. His large round
face with its wide-set eyes leered down at me
like a giant floating balloon that I'd seen in a
Thanksgiving Day parade.

The grin seemed frozen in time. It carried
me back to the night of the accident. Trotter
had been grinning and laughing and teasing.
Then it had happened. The grin had turned to a
look of panic, and he had run. Trotter had run,
leaving me to handle everything. And now he
was home playing basketball while I had to be
cooped up in that tiny little room at the police
station.

Trotter started for his house as I fished my
key out of my jeans pocket.

"Hey, Riley," he called.

I turned around.

"What?" I asked.

"Say hi to my old pal Officer MacDougal for me."

Trotter laughed and shuffled away.

I went into the house and took off my jacket. As I hung it on its hook, I noticed a smear of chocolate on the left arm, where Trotter had punched me.

"Perfect. The stain of Trotter," I said to myself. I took the jacket to the kitchen sink to try to wash it out.

Thursday, September 16

Mitch: Hi, Wootie. It's Mitchell.

MapleG: So you CAN be on time if you try.

Mitch: Yes. How are things at Maple-LESS Grove?

MapleG: Ha! I like that. I'll have to remember it. Things are the same here. That's the problem. Every day is exactly the same as the one before it. I guess the plan is to bore us to death.

Mitch: That's how I feel about school some days.

MapleG: I used to feel that way, too. Now I'd give anything to be back in school. My favorite subject was spelling. I was the school champion in sixth grade. I went on to the countywide competition, but I was eliminated there. I still remember the word I missed. Divisible. I spelled it "-a-b-l-e." I can see that you're a good speller, too.

Mitch: I guess so. My dad always used to ask me my spelling words while he was fixing dinner.

MapleG: Does he still?

Mitch: No. He's working over in Bowmansville for a few months. It's an hour away so he doesn't get back until almost seven o'clock most nights. I hang out and do my homework and stuff until he gets home.

MapleG: What does he do there?

Mitch: He's an assistant foreman at Harrington Radiator. He's filling in at the Bowmansville plant for a foreman who had some kind of surgery.

Maple G: You don't eat dinner until seven o'clock?

Mitch: It's not so bad. Dad leaves me a note telling what to get ready for dinner so that we can eat as soon as he gets home. After dinner we do the dishes together. Sometimes we play a few hands of gin rummy before bed.

MapleG: I like gin rummy, but my favorite card game is pinochle. In fact, Lou and I used to belong to a pinochle club with my sister Rose and her husband, Charlie. We played every Friday night. I miss it, and I miss them. They moved to Florida a few years ago. Lou and I visited them there, but I'm not crazy about the heat. I felt like a big slug the whole time I was there.

Mitch: Did you go to Disney World?

MapleG: No, but we did get to watch a space shuttle launch. It was great!

Mitch: My dad told me that when he was a kid, the whole school would go to the auditorium to watch the space launches on TV.

It occurred to me that I wasn't stopping as much to think of things to write. Having a conversation with Wootie wasn't as hard as I thought it was going to be.

MapleG: Now that you mention it, I think my son's school did that, too. In fact, he wanted to be an astronaut when he grew up.

Mitch: How many kids do you have?

MapleG: Just Patrick. He's a history teacher over in Sherbrooke. That's about ninety miles from here. His wife teaches art there. I have two beautiful granddaughters, Carolyn and Julia.

Mitch: Do you get to see them very often?

MapleG: They come to see me once or twice a month, usually on Sundays. They've never missed a Thanksgiving at my house, either. That's another reason that I've got to get back home.

Mitch: How is your hip doing?

MapleG: It could be better, but it could be worse. Nurse Nag-a-lot says that it will probably take a long time to heal. She's just a little ray of sunshine, isn't she?

Mitch: Maybe you can prove her wrong.

MapleG: With pleasure.

Mitch: I've got to go now. Bye, Wootie.

MapleG: Bye, Mitchell.

‹‹ 4:18 P.M. ››

Back at home I called Mrs. Cooper, our next-door neighbor, to tell her I was there. Last year I'd convinced Dad that I didn't need a baby-sitter after school anymore. He worked out a plan with Mrs. Cooper that I check in with her every day when I get home so that she knows I've arrived safely.

Dad's daily note was lying on the kitchen table. It always has three parts: instructions for dinner, a reminder to do my homework, and a trivia question. I'm supposed to have the answer to the question by the time Dad gets home from work.

The answer can usually be found in the dictionary or in the old set of encyclopedias that are in our living room bookcase. I've been trying to convince Dad that we need a computer. I can tell that he's considering it, but I think he's afraid that I'll spend all of my time after school on it. Anyway, Dad has been asking questions lately that require a little more legwork around the house. I've found recent answers in the phone book (What is the zip code for Bradford?) and even in my parents' wedding album (What color roses did your mother carry on her wedding day?).

Dad had weighted down the note with the salt shaker. I picked it up and read it.

Dear Mitchell,

1. We're having beef stew and salad tonight.
    Don't worry. I'll leave out the peas, since
    you always pick them out anyway. I'll put
    in more of those little onions that you
    like. Peel and cut up three carrots and
    wash the lettuce. I'll pick up some ice
    cream for dessert.

2. Don't forget to do your homework.
    Have you started your book report yet?

3. What was the name of Charles
    Lindbergh's airplane?

I changed into my sweat pants and grabbed
a handful of cheese crackers from the cupboard.
Dad had given me the new Hoops cartridge for
my Electronic Gamester so I sat and played it
at the kitchen table.

< < 5:04 P. M. > >

A little while later I looked at the clock. Dad wouldn't be home for another two hours. This was the time of day that I hated the most. I didn't feel like starting my homework, and there was nothing fun to do by myself. I felt like a prisoner in my own house.

I crumpled Dad's note into a ball and practiced throwing it into the wastepaper basket from different positions in the kitchen. Finally I decided that I'd better get started on my book report.

I worked on it for almost an hour. After that, I turned to Dad's question. This one seemed pretty cut-and-dried. I looked up Lindbergh in the encyclopedia, and sure enough, the answer was right in the caption of the photo. The airplane was called *The Spirit of St. Louis*.

Dad told me once that he has two reasons for his daily trivia question. First, he wants me to learn new things. Second, he wants me to be able to find answers by myself.

I know that there's a third reason, too. He wants to keep me out of trouble while he's not home.

< < 6:32 P. M. > >

I was finished with my homework. It was already dark outside, and Dad would be home in a little while. I went to the kitchen and washed the lettuce. The window over our sink looked out on our backyard. Beyond that was the yard of Mrs. Wheeler, our neighbor from the next street over.

I thought again of the accident and the knot in my stomach tightened. The confused, frightened look on Mrs. Wheeler's face that night still haunted me. I could be sitting in school or walking down the street and her face would appear in my thoughts. I peered out, straining to see if Mrs. Wheeler's lights were on. All I could see was the bright reflection of our kitchen light.

Raising the window, I heard the faint sound of a basketball being bounced from a few doors away. Trotter, I thought.

"It's not fair," I muttered. "It was all *his* fault."

I slammed the window shut. When I did, my own reflection stared back at me. I had to look away.

Tuesday, September 21

Mitch: Hi, Wootie.

MapleG: Hi, Mitchell.

Mitch: What's new?

MapleG: Oh, no you don't. I figured out after our last two chats how you keep asking me questions so that I'll ramble on, and then you don't have to write so much. So today it's my turn to ask questions and your turn to spill it. I'd like to know what happened.

Mitch: What happened when?

MapleG: You know very well what I'm talking about. It might make you feel better to tell me about it.

Mitch: It's just that it was a really dumb thing to do.

MapleG: We all do dumb things, believe me. Most of the time we can't change them, so we learn from them and go on from there.

Mitch: What did you ever do that was dumb?

MapleG: Lots of things. Probably the dumbest was the time I . . . oh. Nice try. We're talking about YOU today, remember?

Mitch: It almost worked.

MapleG: Very funny. Keep going.

Mitch: Well, it all started when my friend Michael moved to Chicago. I didn't have anyone to hang around with this summer.

MapleG: Go on.

Mitch: So I started hanging around with this kid

named Trotter. He was new to the neighborhood last year. I know he's a complete jerk, but I started hanging around with him, anyway.

MapleG: What makes him such a jerk?

Mitch: Let's put it this way. The first time I ever met him, he was teasing the Coopers' dog, Lady. She was chained up to a post. The chain was pretty long, but Trotter was putting dog biscuits just out of Lady's reach. He just sat there and laughed while Lady went crazy barking and tugging on her chain.

MapleG: You're right. He is a complete jerk.

Mitch: I know, but he was good for a laugh sometimes. It seemed better than hanging around by myself all the time. Anyway, there's an old lady who lives on the street behind us. Her yard backs up to our yard. Her name is Mrs. Wheeler.

MapleG: An OLD lady? Watch it, buster.

Mitch: Sorry. I just think of her as ancient because even when I was little she seemed really old. She's kind of mean, too. Once, a ball of mine went into her yard. I saw her pick it up and lock it in her toolshed. I never did get it back. Another time, I fell off my bike onto her front lawn and she yelled at me. I FELL, for crying out loud. On Halloween, she always turned off all her lights and pretended she wasn't home. We could see the curtains move, so we knew she was looking out at us.

MapleG: Maybe she's afraid.

Mitch: Maybe. I think she's just mean. OOPS. Officer Mac just gave me the signal that our time is up. I've got to go.

MapleG: Will you finish your story Thursday?

Mitch: I'll try. Bye.

I was relieved that the time was up. It was hard to write about what had happened that

night. And wasn't telling the truth what got me
here in the first place?

<< 4:10 P.M. >>

"How's everything going at Maple Grove?"
Officer Mac asked on the way home.

"Okay," I answered. "My O.L.D. Friend
seems nice. In fact, she's actually kind of funny."

I told Officer Mac about Wootie and Nurse
Nag-a-lot.

He laughed and said, "I'm glad it's going
well."

Then he glanced over at me.

"Mitchell, you haven't been hanging around
Trotter lately, have you?"

"Not if I can help it," I said. I looked at
Officer Mac. I wasn't sure if he believed me, so I
went on. "Sometimes he's just there. If I try to
get rid of him he's even more of a pest. He's like
a fly. The more you swat at it, the more it
bothers you. You have to let it go away by itself.
That's what I usually do with Trotter."

Officer Mac grinned.

"Sounds like you're handling it just right," he said.

I'd be handling it better if Trotter was being punished, I thought.

Officer Mac must have been thinking about that, too, because he said, "I wish we could have convinced Trotter's mother to put him in the O.L.D. Friend program. It might have done him some good."

I didn't say anything.

Officer Mac stopped the car at the corner. He looked at me and said, "You may not think so right now, Mitchell, but your father only wanted to do what's best for you."

"Okay, what if I told you that I've learned my lesson?" I asked, turning toward Officer Mac. "I've thought and thought about what happened, and I know I'll never do anything so stupid again. Do I still have to come back on Thursday?"

"A few minutes ago you told me that it's going well," said Officer Mac.

I looked out the window and thought about my conversation with Wootie.

"It's okay," I said. "I just don't see why I have to come back if I've learned my lesson."

I started to open the car door.

"Just a minute, Mitchell," said Officer Mac. "You say you've learned your lesson, right?"

"Yes," I said.

Officer Mac paused.

"Then how can you think of quitting the program? Has it occurred to you that this program might be important to Wootie Hayes? Maybe you should think about it from her point of view."

"Can't you just assign someone else to be her O.L.D. Friend?" I asked.

Officer Mac stared at me.

"Is that what being a *friend* means to you?" he asked.

I looked away.

We just sat there for a minute. Finally Officer Mac asked, "So how about it? Will I see you on Thursday?"

I looked at him, and then I nodded.

"Good man," said Officer Mac, offering me a handshake.

I shook his hand and climbed out of the car.

"Hey, Mitchell," Officer Mac called.

I bent over and looked back into the car at him.

"Yeah?" I asked.

Officer Mac smiled and said, "You really don't think your dad would have let you quit the program, anyway, do you?"

"You're probably right," I said, closing the car door. I waved and headed for home.

< < 4:20 P. M. > >

When I walked up the driveway a few minutes later, Trotter was just coming around the side of our garage. He looked startled when he saw me.

"Time for pest control," I muttered to myself.

"Hey, it's Really Riley!" Trotter called.

"Hey, Trotter," I answered.

"Wanna shoot some hoops?" he asked.

"No thanks. I've got to vacuum the house."

Trotter groaned. "You're always doing chores. Didn't your old man hear that slavery was abolished?"

"Don't you ever have chores to do?"
I asked.

Trotter laughed. "Are you kidding me?
Whenever my mom used to ask me to do
anything around the house, I'd either
deliberately mess it up or take forever to do it.
Once I vacuumed right over a ballpoint pen that
was on the living room floor. It broke apart and
got ink all over the rug. I pretended that I
hadn't seen it."

He smirked, and went on.

"The best one was when I flushed a rubber
glove down the toilet. We had to have a plumber
come to get it out. After that, Mom never asked
me to help again. You oughta try it."

"I'll keep that in mind," I said, unlocking the
door to our house.

Trotter bounced the basketball.

"How about after dinner?" he asked.

"Can't," I answered. "I've got to work on
my science project."

"Loser," Trotter said.

"I've got to go," I said, opening the door.

Trotter dribbled the ball down the driveway. I went upstairs to change my clothes.

‹ ‹ 4:31 P. M. › ›

I heard the sound of a lawn mower starting up. I glanced out of my bedroom window. Mrs. Trotman was mowing their backyard. Trotter was back in his driveway practicing his lay-ups.

"What a guy," I thought to myself as I hauled the vacuum cleaner out of the closet.

Thursday, September 23

< < 3:30 P. M. > >

Mitch: Hi, Wootie. How are you?

MapleG: I'm fine. Now let's skip the small talk and get back to your story. At this rate, the snow will fall before I hear what happened.

Mitch: I forgot what I told you so far.

MapleG: Michael moved away. Trotter is a jerk. Mrs. Wheeler lives behind you. She's old and she's mean. That about sums it up.

So much for my plan to stall for a little time, I thought. I took a deep breath and began to type.

Mitch: Okay. Mrs. Wheeler had a cat named Fluffy. Isn't that a dumb name for a cat?

I mean, the cat did have fluffy fur and everything, but she could have come up with something more original.

MapleG: I used to have a cat named Boots. He was white with four black paws. Does that meet with your approval?

Mitch: Sure. That's a good cat name. Anyway, Mrs. Wheeler loved that cat. I'd always see her in the backyard combing Fluffy or playing with her. They took naps together in the lawn chair. I'd hear Mrs. Wheeler talking to her all the time, too. She'd say things like, "Aren't our tulips beautiful this year, Fluffy?" or, "What shall we fix for dinner tonight, Fluffy?" I could just picture Fluffy sitting up to the dining room table with a little bib tied around his neck.

MapleG: Is this leading somewhere?

Mitch: I'm getting there. At the beginning of summer, Fluffy disappeared. I'd hear Mrs. Wheeler calling for her every night. She even went around to all the neighbors asking if anyone had seen Fluffy. She seemed desperate to get her back.

MapleG: The poor woman. Sounds like she lost one of her best friends.

Mitch: I guess so. Anyway, one night in July, my dad had to work a double shift. Trotter came over after dinner to shoot basketball. Dad had told me not to leave the house, but I figured it would be okay if I just stayed in our yard. It was pretty dark.

I stopped typing. It wasn't that I didn't remember what happened next. I had replayed the scene in my head so many times that I knew it by heart. I was just hard to type the words.

MapleG: Yes?

Mitchell: Okay. All of a sudden, we heard Mrs. Wheeler calling Fluffy. At first Trotter said,

"Why doesn't she give it up?" Then he laughed and said, "Come on. I've got an idea." I followed Trotter over into the bushes that separate Mrs. Wheeler's yard from ours. I could see her standing on her back steps. She sounded really pathetic.

I stopped again. My hands were sweaty so I wiped them on my pants and went on:

The next time she called Fluffy, Trotter winked at me and meowed back. You could see Mrs. Wheeler really perk up her ears at that, so Trotter meowed again. Mrs. Wheeler called, "Fluffy? Is that you?" She came to the edge of the back steps and called again. Trotter meowed a few more times. We saw Mrs. Wheeler start to come toward us. After that, I'm not really sure what happened. I guess she couldn't see very well in the dark or she lost her balance, because she fell all the way down the steps.

MapleG: Oh, dear. What did you do?

Mitch: Well, Trotter didn't stick around. By the time Mrs. Wheeler hit the ground, he was off and running for home. I stood there for a few seconds. I could see Mrs. Wheeler trying to sit up, but she seemed to be having trouble. I ran back to my house and called 911. Then I went back through the bushes and over to Mrs. Wheeler. She was moaning, and I could see blood on her forehead. I was really scared that she was going to die. Then I heard sirens. Pretty soon, the ambulance came, and so did the police. They asked me what happened, and I was so scared that I told them everything. The paramedics were working on Mrs. Wheeler, so she heard the whole thing, too. After they took her away in the ambulance the police brought me home. Dad was just getting there from work.

MapleG: What happened?

Mitch: He was furious with me. Officer MacDougal made me tell him the whole story. He also went to Trotter's house to get his version of the story. Later, Officer Mac told my dad that Trotter had pinned the whole thing on me. Since it wasn't really a crime we didn't get charged with anything. That's when Officer Mac told my dad about the O.L.D. Friend program. Dad thought it was a good idea, so here I am. I was also grounded for the rest of the month. Since Trotter blamed everything on me, his mother didn't make him sign up for the program.

MapleG: What happened to Mrs. Wheeler?

Mitch: Dad found out that she broke her wrist and had a cut on her head that took three stitches. I saw her out in the yard last week. She seems to be okay. Dad made me write an apology note to her.

MapleG: What did she say when you gave it to her?

I hesitated, then I wrote:

Nothing. I just put the note in her mailbox and came home. I still get a big knot in my stomach

when I even look at her yard. And it's pretty
hard not to, since it's right behind my house.

MapleG: Maybe the knot would go away if you
talked to her. Besides, it seems like you're being
awfully hard on yourself. Trotter is really the
one who caused the accident, not you.

I was sweating all over now. I sat there, not
typing for a while.

MapleG: Mitchell?

I took a deep breath. Slowly I typed.

Mitch: Wootie, there's something I left out of
my story.

MapleG: What's that?

Mitch: I meowed, too.

MapleG: I see.

I waited for more words to follow. Just then Officer Mac poked his head into the room.

"I've got to go out on a call, Mitchell. It's time to wrap things up for today anyway."

I nodded.

Mitch: Wootie, Officer Mac just told me that my time's up. I'll talk to you again on Tuesday, okay? I've really got to go now, okay?

MapleG: Okay.

Mitch: Bye, Wootie.

I waited for a goodbye message from Wootie, but it didn't come.

‹ ‹ 4:17 P. M. › ›

I was hoping to talk to Officer Mac on my way home, but he was already gone. Another officer gave me a ride.

It started raining as I headed home from the corner. I hadn't thought to bring a jacket that morning. The rain soaked through my T-shirt in no time, and the sharp wind made me feel cold to the bone. My backpack was loaded down with some extra books that I had borrowed from the library for the science project.

The knot in my stomach was tighter than ever. Why should I care what Wootie thought of me? I had never even met the woman. I certainly didn't need her judging me.

I was shivering by the time I unlocked the door to our house. Luckily, Trotter wasn't hanging around. The rain would probably keep him in front of the television all afternoon.

I headed upstairs to change out of my wet clothes. I put on some sweats. It felt good to be warm and dry. Sitting on the edge of my bed, I pulled on a pair of clean socks.

My mom's picture stared at me from its frame on top of my bedside table. I picked it up and looked at it. Mom was wearing a pale blue sweater and a string of pearls. Her dark brown hair hung to her shoulders. Everything in the picture had a slight fuzziness around the edges, making Mom's sweater and hair look extra soft.

I didn't remember much about my mother, but my dad had told me lots of stories about her. My favorite story was about the time that Mom gave Dad a haircut. I used to ask Dad to tell the story over and over. It seems that my parents were trying to save money to buy the house, and Mom thought that she could do as well as a barber could. She ended up giving Dad a really bad haircut.

The next day when he came home from work, Mom was cooking at the stove. When she turned around, she was wearing a fake mustache. She told him that if he had to look silly because of her, then she would look silly, too. They had a good laugh over it. Later, they went out for ice cream and Mom wore the mustache.

Dad told me once that the haircut story pretty much summed up how Mom saw things. She couldn't stand it when people said "If only I'd done this, or if only I'd done that." She believed in facing up to a bad situation and then moving on. Dad said that's what helped him get on with life after Mom died.

I couldn't help thinking that if only I'd never met Trotter, I wouldn't be in such a bad situation. If only everyone would see that the whole thing was his fault, I'd be able to move on. *If only . . .*

Tuesday, September 28

< < 3:30 P. M. > >

Mitch: Hi, Wootie. It's me.

MapleG: Mitchell, this is Wallace. Wootie can't make it today. She's not feeling very well.

Mitch: What's wrong with her?

MapleG: I don't know if I should tell you this, but Wootie has some other health problems besides her hip.

Mitch: Like what?

MapleG: She has heart trouble. She caught a bad cold, and her doctor wanted her to stay in bed today. Her eyesight is starting to go, too.

It looks like she might not be able to go back to her home. It would be too dangerous for her to live alone.

Mitch: Does Wootie know that?

MapleG: I'm not sure. She hasn't said much about it.

I thought of my last conversation with Wootie. I wondered if she was mad at me. Maybe she wanted to quit the program after finding out about Mrs. Wheeler.

Mitch: Wallace, did Wootie say anything after our last chat?

MapleG: She was actually pretty quiet when I took her back to her room. Mitchell, she looks forward to your chats more than anything else here. Knowing her, she'll be furious about having to miss today.

Mitch: You really think so?

MapleG: I know so. I've got to go now.

Mitch: Bye, Wallace. And thanks.

‹ ‹ 3:45 P. M. › ›

I thought about Wootie all the way home.
It had never occurred to me that she might have
problems other than her hip. What if
she couldn't go back to her house? She'd be
miserable living at Maple-less Grove forever.

Officer Mac dropped me off at the corner as
usual. I don't know what made me do it, but
instead of going straight home I walked around
the block to Mrs. Wheeler's street. I hesitated,
then turned down the street until I was almost
in front of her home. Standing in the shadow of a
huge oak tree, I looked at the house.

Royal blue shutters stood out sharply against
the weathered gray boards that sided the house.
A porch swing, painted the same
bold blue, moved slightly in the wind. A brick
walk led up to the front steps.

Behind the house I could see the toolshed in

Mrs. Wheeler's yard. At the very back of the lot stood a row of bushes. Beyond that, I could see our house. I realized that I had never seen this view of our place before.

Suddenly the front door of Mrs. Wheeler's house opened. I stepped quickly behind the tree. After a few seconds, I peeked carefully around.

Mrs. Wheeler walked out onto the porch. She took a broom that was standing in the corner and swept the dried leaves off the porch. Pulling her sweater more tightly around her shoulders, she stood for a few moments looking around at the neighborhood. A neighbor who was raking leaves next door called to her. Mrs. Wheeler waved.

I had been thinking of Wootie, and about how much she must miss the house that she had lived in for years. Now, as I watched Mrs. Wheeler, I realized that she'd probably feel the same way. I couldn't picture Mrs. Wheeler living any place else. As I was watching, she took the newspaper from its box next to the front door and went back inside.

I stood frozen behind the tree for a few minutes. Finally I stepped out from the shadow

of the tree and hurried around the block to
our house. As soon as I was inside I called Mrs.
Cooper to let her know that I was home.

<< 9:04 P. M. >>

Later that night Dad and I were playing
cards.

"How was Wootie today?" Dad asked.

"We didn't get to have our chat," I answered,
explaining about Wootie's cold.

I hadn't told him much about our last chat.
I still wondered what Wootie thought of me
after I told her about Mrs. Wheeler's fall.

Dad shuffled the cards for another hand.

"Wootie sounds a lot like my Grandma
Riley," he said. "She lived right next door to
us while I was growing up, so I spent a lot of
time with her. She was quite a lady."

Dad stopped shuffling and chuckled.

"When I was in sixth grade, I fell out of a
tree and broke my arm. It was a week before
final exams. I couldn't write a word. The
teacher told me that I would have to just do the

best I could with my left hand. When Grandma Riley heard that, she marched into the principal's office and asked her to kindly provide a room where I could take the exam by dictating my answers to someone else. The principal agreed to do that, and I took the exams in the Health Office with the school nurse doing the writing for me."

"How did you do on the exams?" I asked.

"Pretty well," Dad replied. He set the deck of cards on the table.

"I wish you'd had a chance to get to know your own grandparents, Mitch. It would be nice for you to have someone like Grandma Riley around while I'm at work. I can't help feeling that by not being here, I'm a little responsible for what happened to Mrs. Wheeler. I guess I shouldn't have left you here by yourself."

"That's not true, Dad," I protested. "I'm old enough to be by myself. I just never should have listened to Trotter. I could have refused to go along with him, but..." I stopped. "But I didn't, so it was my fault, too."

Dad looked at me.

"I'm glad you figured that out," he said.

He stood up and stretched.

"Ready to turn in?" he asked.

"I'll be up in a minute," I answered.

After Dad went upstairs, I sat at the table thinking about what I'd said to him. I had told him that he wasn't to blame for the accident, and that it was my fault for following Trotter's lead.

Saying it out loud to Dad like that had made it sound like the truth. *Was* I partly to blame? All along I had been blaming Trotter, but the more I thought about it, the more I had to admit that it really was my fault, too, for going along with him.

< < 9:39 P. M. > >

While I lay in bed I looked at my mother's picture bathed in moonlight. I thought about the haircut story and pictured my mother with a fake mustache. Make the best of a bad situation and then move on. *Make the best of a bad situation.* I hadn't quite done that yet. How could I, when I hadn't even faced the truth about that night? Maybe if I finally accepted the fact that it *was* my fault for going along with Trotter, I *could* move on. For some strange reason I felt relieved when I thought about what I had to do.

Thursday, September 30
< < 3:30 P. M. > >

Mitch: Hi, Wootie. Are you there?

MapleG: Where else would I be?

Mitch: Is your cold better?

MapleG: Yes it is, thank you very much. I take it Mr. Big Mouth Wallace told you all about it?

Mitch: Technically, it didn't take a big mouth to type it on a keyboard. Mr. Big Fingers, maybe?

MapleG: Don't be a wise guy. What else did he tell you?

Mitch: Only that Nurse Nag-a-lot is really the sweetest, kindest lady on the face of the earth. He just can't figure out why you two don't get along.

MapleG: Careful. She could creep up behind us at any time.

Mitch: I was thinking, Wootie. Maybe if you like pinochle so much, you could start up a club like you used to belong to. I know you can get cards with big numbers on them for people with bad eyesight.

Wootie didn't respond for a couple of minutes. I realized that I had probably said too much about what Wallace had told me.

MapleG: Who said anything about bad eyesight?

Mitch: I just mean that there might be some people there who can't see so well anymore.

MapleG: It would be better than idiotic BINGO.

Mitch: You could give BIG boxes of tissues for your prizes. Maybe even rolls of paper towels for the tournaments.

MapleG: Very funny. Anyway, I don't plan on being here that long. Why are you in such rare form today?

Mitch: I've been thinking about what you said.

MapleG: What's that?

Mitch: You said that my stomach knot might go away if I talk to Mrs. Wheeler.

MapleG: It might be worth a try.

Mitch: I'm not sure what to say to her.

MapleG: I'd just tell her that you'd like a chance to explain what happened. Then tell the story just the way you told me. Leave out the part about her being mean, though. And I would end it with two little words that are sometimes very hard to say.

Mitch: "I'm sorry?"

MapleG: Those are the ones. Mitchell, did Trotter apologize to Mrs. Wheeler?

Mitch: Are you kidding me?

MapleG: Then this is your chance to prove that you're not a complete jerk like him.

Mitch: Thanks, Wootie. Oh, I almost forgot to tell you that there's a space shuttle launch scheduled for Monday morning. Do they let you watch TV there?

MapleG: That's one thing they DO let us do. I'll be sure to watch it, thanks. That gives me two things to look forward to. Patrick and Lisa and the girls are coming on Sunday to spend the day with me.

Mitch: That's great.

MapleG: Is our time up?

Mitch: Just about. And don't forget about the pinochle idea.

MapleG: We'll see. Good luck with Mrs. Wheeler.

Mitch: Thanks. Bye.

‹‹ 4:10 P.M. ››

Officer Mac dropped me off. The little room in the police station had been hot and stuffy. Once outside, I breathed in the cool, crisp autumn air. The leaves had begun to change color, and some of them were starting to fall.

I had pretty much decided to talk to Mrs. Wheeler sometime over the weekend. The hard part would be getting up the nerve to ring her doorbell. Once she answered, there would be no turning back anyway.

Now that my decision was made, I felt better than I had in weeks. I was whistling as I started up the driveway. Turning the key to unlock our back door, I heard Trotter's voice.

"Hey, it's Really Riley," he panted, loping up from the side of our garage. His face was streaked with grease, and several leaves were stuck in his hair.

I looked at Trotter and then at the garage.

"What were you doing, Trotter?" I asked.

"Oh, my basketball went into the bushes by your garage. I was just retrieving it."

"Oh," I said. "Well, I'll see you. I've got a lot of homework to do."

"Yeah. Me, too," said Trotter. "I'd better get at it. See ya."

I went inside and called Mrs. Cooper to tell her I was home.

< < 4:28 P.M. > >

I read Dad's note:

Dear Mitch,

1. We're having macaroni and cheese tonight. Grate two cups of cheddar cheese into a bowl. Bring a can of green beans

and some applesauce up from the cellar. We'll have ice cream for dessert.

2. Don't you have a social studies test to study for?

3. Where is the Basketball Hall of Fame?

I changed my clothes and made myself a peanut butter sandwich. While I was eating it, I flipped through the channels on TV. There wasn't anything good on, so I sorted baseball cards for a while.

< < 5:25 P. M. > >

I went to the encyclopedia to look up the answer to Dad's question. I found out that the Basketball Hall of Fame is in Springfield, Massachusetts. I looked at the picture of a player dribbling a ball. Something clicked in my head.

Trotter had said that he was looking for his basketball in our bushes, yet he didn't have it with him when he left. He'd been hanging around the yard a lot lately. Even more suspicious was the fact that he had been in a hurry to do his homework.

I went out onto the back steps. It was already getting dark. The neighborhood was quiet, except for the sound of a basketball being bounced. Beyond Mrs. Cooper's yard, the light on Trotter's garage shone on his driveway. There he was, practicing his dribbling.

So much for the missing basketball, I thought. And what about all of that homework Trotter had to do? He couldn't be done with it already. I had a feeling that he was up to something.

It probably wasn't good.

I had made up my mind to talk to Mrs. Wheeler after school. I stopped home to drop off my backpack, and then headed over to her house before I could change my mind.

At one time I would have cut across her backyard, but I didn't feel right about it anymore. Instead, I went around the block and rang her front doorbell. She didn't answer the door. I could have sworn that I saw the living room curtains move, but still no one answered. After a minute or so, I started to leave. As I was going down the sidewalk, I heard the door open.

"What do you want?" Mrs. Wheeler called.

I turned around and looked at her. "Uh. I just wanted a chance to explain what happened," I stammered. "You know, the night you fell?"

Mrs. Wheeler squinted and looked at me for a few seconds. I braced myself, expecting her to yell at me or to kick me off her property. Instead she motioned toward the porch swing and said, "Sit down."

I climbed the steps and sat down. Mrs. Wheeler came out and sat on a plastic lawn chair. She was wearing black pants and a sweatshirt that had autumn leaves stenciled on the front. Her skin, crisscrossed with wrinkles, seemed almost transparent. Her white hair was cut short, and I could see a scar on her forehead, probably from the accident. She seemed smaller than I remembered. She sat there, not saying anything, so I finally took a deep breath and plunged in. I told her the whole story.

"I'm really sorry, Mrs. Wheeler," I said finally.

She still didn't say anything. I figured by her silence that I was dismissed, so I started to get up from the swing.

Mrs. Wheeler said suddenly, "I should have known all along that it wasn't Fluffy."

I sat back down on the swing as she went on. "It didn't even sound like her."

"Did you ever find out what happened to her?" I asked.

Mrs. Wheeler shook her head. "She was almost fourteen years old. She hadn't been herself for a few days. I think that she probably went away to die."

Neither of us said anything for a little while. Then Mrs. Wheeler leaned forward in her chair. "Would you like to see a picture of her?" she asked.

"Sure," I said.

Mrs. Wheeler went inside, and came back with a picture of two white cats.

"That's Fluffy when she was only a few years old," she explained. "The other one was Long John Silver. See that black patch around his eye?"

"That's a great name for him," I said.

Mrs. Wheeler smiled. "He was a frisky one. Fluffy was much more prim and proper."

"Do you think you'll get another cat?" I asked.

Mrs. Wheeler looked at the picture of the two cats.

"At first I didn't think so," she said. "But I do miss the company." She laughed. "I'm sure you used to hear me talking to Fluffy all the time. She was a very good listener. I've been thinking lately that a little kitten would be nice to have around. I'll probably go to the animal pound sometime next week to pick one out."

Mrs. Wheeler hesitated, then she spoke.

"The truth is, Mitchell, I don't really like being by myself. I don't think I'll ever get used to it."

I nodded. Mrs. Wheeler went on. "The neighborhood has changed so much since my husband died. It scares me to be here alone sometimes. I probably haven't been a very friendly neighbor, but I've had problems with some of the kids in the neighborhood. Sometimes it's easier if I just lock the doors and keep to myself."

I remembered the time Mrs. Wheeler had locked my ball in her toolshed, and when she had yelled at me for falling off my bike. I thought about her turning off her lights on Halloween night.

"If you're ever scared, you could just call Dad or me," I offered.

Mrs. Wheeler smiled.

"I'll remember that," she said.

"Well, I'd better be going now," I said. "Thanks for showing me your picture and everything."

We both stood up. I was a few inches taller than Mrs. Wheeler. She looked up at me and said, "Goodbye, Mitchell. Come back next week and see my new kitten."

"I will. Bye, Mrs. Wheeler."

‹ ‹ 4:38 P. M. › ›

On the way home, it occurred to me that Wootie had been right. Mrs. Wheeler was just afraid.

As I unlocked the back door, I heard the phone ringing. I ran to answer it.

"Mitchell?"

I recognized Mrs. Wheeler's voice.

"Yes?" I answered.

"Next time, why don't you cut through the

backyard instead of going all the way around the block?" she asked, chuckling.

"Thanks. I'll do that," I said.

We said goodbye. I would keep my promise to visit Mrs. Wheeler again. In fact, I was actually looking forward to it.

Tuesday, October 5

<< 3:31 P. M. >>

Mitch: Hi, Wootie.

MapleG: Hi, Mitchell. Well?

Mitch: I did it. I went to Mrs. Wheeler's house on Friday after school. I had to force myself to do it, but I did it. It wasn't nearly as bad as I thought it would be.

MapleG: Tell me all about it.

I was so eager to tell Wootie about my visit with Mrs. Wheeler that my fingers couldn't keep up with my brain. I kept making typing mistakes and had to go back a couple of times to fix them. I ended by telling Wootie that Mrs. Wheeler had invited me back again.

MapleG: If you were here, I'd give you a big hug.

Mitch: If I were there, I might even let you.

MapleG: Did the knot go away?

Mitch: I haven't really thought about it, so I guess it must have. My dad was pretty happy about the whole thing, too. He told me that he knew all along that I had just put the apology letter in her mailbox. He said that he knew I'd do the right thing when I was ready.

MapleG: I'm so glad.

Mitch: How was your visit with the family?

MapleG: Wonderful, but too short. We went for a drive in the country and stopped for hot fudge sundaes on the way back. The girls were little chatterboxes. It was so good to see them. It made me want to get out of here even more. I have to call my doctor this week to find out how I'm really doing. They never tell me anything here, you know.

Mitch: I hope it's good news.

MapleG: Thank you. Did you watch the space shuttle launch?

Mitch: No. I asked my math teacher first period if we could wheel in a TV to watch it, but he said we had to review for the chapter test this week.

MapleG: It seems to me you can have a chapter test any day. How often can you watch a space shuttle launch?

Mitch: That's what I thought, but he won out. How was it?

MapleG: It was a good one. I watched it in the sitting room with a lady whose grandson works for NASA. We had ourselves a good old time. We ate dinner together last night, too. Her name is Fran.

Mitch: That's great. I've got to go now, Wootie. Bye.

MapleG: Bye. And Mitchell, I'm proud of you.

< < 4:29 P. M. > >

I went to my room to change into my sweats. I was planning to make some microwave popcorn and watch a National League play-off game on TV. My room felt hot and stuffy so I went over to crack open my window. A flash of movement caught my eye. Trotter was crossing our neighbor's backyard and heading toward our garage.

He was almost to our driveway when I heard his mother call him in for supper. Trotter looked annoyed. He glanced toward his house, and then back at our garage. Mrs. Trotman called out again. Trotter hesitated, and then headed back toward his house. Something was up.

< < 4:48 P. M. > >

It was almost dark as I closed the back porch door behind me. I crossed the yard and walked behind the garage. The bushes there were thick and overgrown. I crouched down, trying to see through the tangled mass of leaves and branches. I couldn't see much.

Walking around to the far back corner of the garage, I noticed a narrow passageway between the bushes and the building. I could see something shiny about four feet in. Squeezing through the opening, I looked closer.

A bright orange mountain bike was propped against the garage. It had black tiger stripes painted on the crossbar and a double water bottle holder. I had seen one exactly like it in the yard of a house two streets over. My heart pounded inside my chest. Trotter's mom could never afford to buy a bike like this. There was only one explanation that I could think of for the bike being there, and now it was on *our* property.

I looked around to make sure that Trotter wasn't anywhere in sight, then I hurried back to the house. Trotter would be eating dinner for a while, and Dad probably wouldn't be home for at least an hour. I paced back and forth in the kitchen trying to decide what to do next. Finally I came up with a plan. I went to collect the things that I needed. I hoped that I knew Trotter as well as I thought I did.

‹ ‹ 6:32 P. M. › ›

A little while later I was sitting on the back steps. By then it was completely dark. I was looking up at the sky, trying to find the Big Dipper, when I heard someone moving through the bushes by the garage. Then I saw a dark shape coming toward me.

"Hey, Trotter," I said quietly.

He stopped. I could tell that I'd startled him.

"What did you do with it, Riley?" he asked, moving toward me again.

"With what?" I asked.

"You know what."

"No. Really I don't."

"Quit playing games," Trotter snarled. "Where is the bike?"

"Oh, that," I answered. "It's someplace safe. Don't worry about it."

"Get it now," demanded Trotter.

"I think we'll just leave it where it is for tonight," I said.

Trotter took a step closer. "I want my bike," he growled.

"*Your* bike?" I asked. "I know that it came from over on Walnut Street, Trotter. There can't be too many bikes like that around. So how did you do it?"

Trotter narrowed his eyes and looked at me for a few moments. Then he shrugged.

"I guess I can always deny it if you decide to rat me out. It was a piece of cake, Riley. The bike was leaning against the front steps of that big gray house on Walnut. I was coming home from the store one night and saw it. It was dark and no one was around, so I rode it home. I figure anyone who leaves a bike like that laying around deserves to have it stolen."

"You would think that," I said.

Trotter took another step closer to me.

"Look, moron. If you touched it, your fingerprints are all over it. If I don't get my bike, it won't bother me one bit to see you go down for this all by yourself."

"You mean like I did for Mrs. Wheeler's accident?"

Trotter laughed.

"Yeah, that's right. And with that little episode in your background, the police won't have any trouble believing that you're involved in stealing bikes."

I stood up.

"You know Trotter," I said. "Your name suits you perfectly. A trotter is someone who runs. So why don't you run on home. But first you might like to know that I'm taping this whole conversation."

Trotter stopped and looked around. I pointed to our screened porch. I held my breath as Trotter walked over to the screen and peered in. My old cassette player sat in the corner on a little stool. There was just enough moonlight for us to be able to see the tape winding around and around on its spindle.

Trotter tried to open the door to the porch, but it was locked. He rattled the door and then turned back to me. Grabbing my shoulders, he threw me to the ground. He knelt beside me and raised his arm to punch me.

"Go ahead, Trotter," I said, trying to keep my voice steady. "Go ahead and hit me. That'll prove what a man you are."

Trotter lowered his fist and grabbed my sweatshirt. He pulled me up by the cloth until his face was close to mine.

"It's better than being a little rat who runs squealing to the police or his daddy," he growled.

Trotter and I stared at each other. Suddenly he slammed me back down on the ground. He let go of my shirt and sat back on his knees. I lay there looking up at him.

"So what were you planning to do with the bike?" I asked. "You can't ride it around here without someone recognizing it."

"No kidding. I was planning to sell it, moron."

Trotter closed his eyes. When he opened them, they shone with tears. He blinked and turned away.

"What do you want from me, Riley?" he

asked, wiping his eyes with his sleeve.

"I want you to take the bike back to where you got it," I replied, scrambling to my feet. "If you don't, the tape goes to the police. I know some kids on that street, and I'll find out if you don't take it back. Deal?"

Trotter stared at me for a long time and then stood up. He nodded.

I reached out my hand and he shook it. Just then, the lights from Dad's car shone on the driveway. I heard the car door slam.

"I'll put the bike by the side of the garage when I take the garbage out later," I told Trotter, unlocking the porch door with my key.

Dad came around the corner of the house. I could tell that he was surprised to see me standing there with Trotter.

"Hi, guys. What's up?" Dad asked cautiously. I looked at Trotter.

"I wondered if Riley might want to shoot a little basketball under the lights," said Trotter.

"Well, Trotter," said Dad. "It's a little late for that tonight. Mitchell and I have to go in and eat dinner. Maybe another time?"

"Sure," answered Trotter. "Well, I'd better get home."

He started to walk away.

"Hey, Trotter," I called.

He turned around.

"Yeah?"

I looked at him. I wanted to let Trotter know that I wasn't going to forget about our deal.

"That house we were talking about? It's on Walnut Street."

Trotter nodded. He turned and walked away.

I followed Dad into the house. He didn't notice my cassette player sitting in the corner. I went over and pushed the stop button, breathing a sigh of relief. I had taken a chance on Trotter not looking too closely at the machine. What he didn't know was that it didn't even have a record feature. One of my dad's old Beatles tapes had been playing in the machine with the volume turned all the way down.

Thursday, October 7
<< 3:30 P. M. >>

Mitch: Hi, Wootie.

MapleG: Hi, Mitchell.

Mitch: What's new at Maple-less Grove?

MapleG: Lots. For one thing, it turns out that
Nurse Nag-a-lot was right about my hip.
I talked to the doctor, and it's not mending all
that well. I don't know which is worse, having a
bad hip or having Nurse Nag-a-lot be right.

Mitch: Does that mean you're stuck there?

MapleG: No. That's the good news. Patrick and
Lisa have my name on a waiting list for a place

right there in Sherbrooke. It's one of those assisted living homes where you have your own apartment, but someone is there to check on you and help you with things. My house is for sale, and apparently someone is already interested in it.

Mitch: Are you upset about it?

MapleG: Yes. But as much as I love that house, I'd rather be near my family. They can pop in to see me any time they want, and I can visit them if I'm up to it. I've had lots of time to think in this place. I know that I can't live by myself anymore. My heart flutters and my eyes are getting bad, not to mention my bum hip. My house needs someone who can take proper care of it. I just can't keep up with the work anymore. I know that Lou would understand if he was here. Patrick is going to drive me over there next week so that I can decide what to get rid of and what to keep. Besides, I have lots of memories tucked away in my head and in my photo albums. I guess it's time to move on.

Mitch: Speaking of that, Officer Mac told me today that I only have one chat left with you. Someone else will be taking this spot next Thursday.

MapleG: Has it been a month already?

Mitch: Yes. I can't believe it, either. The first day I came here, I was worried that I'd never be able to chat for thirty minutes.

MapleG: I wasn't too thrilled about the whole thing, either, you know. I didn't like the idea of talking to someone through a computer instead of face-to-face. It was something that Nurse Nag-a-lot said that finally convinced me to try it.

Mitch: Really? What did she say?

MapleG: She said that she didn't blame me for not wanting to chat with some rotten little loser. That's when I said, "Sign me up." I set out to prove her wrong. And I guess I did.

Mitch: Thanks, Wootie. I'm glad you decided to do it.

MapleG: Mitchell, you helped my knot go away, too.

Mitch: What do you mean?

MapleG: I'd had a knot in my stomach since the day I moved in here. I guess I was being pretty stubborn about wanting to go home. Then it occurred to me that if you were brave enough to face Mrs. Wheeler then I could face the truth about my health. And the simple truth is that I can't go home again.

Mitch: I hope it works out for you. Well, it's time to go. I'll be back Tuesday. Bye, Wootie.

MapleG: Until Tuesday, Mitchell.

< < 4:05 P. M. > >

Officer Mac and I walked out into the parking lot.

"How's your computer friend doing?" he asked.

"I'm not so sure," I answered. I described Wootie's medical problems. "It looks like she may not be going back to her house."

"Hmmm. I hope everything goes all right for her."

"I just wish I could do something special for Wootie," I said. "She really helped me work out something that was bothering me."

"Well, if it means anything to you, the O.L.D. Friend Program Coordinator is getting very positive reports back from the Maple Grove Nursing Home Director. According to him, Mrs. Hayes looks forward to your chats very much. Apparently her attitude has improved a lot since you two started communicating."

I still couldn't believe that the time had gone by so quickly.

"It never even occurred to me that I'd have to say goodbye to Wootie."

"You could always write to her," Officer Mac suggested. "I'm not allowed to give out Mrs. Hayes's address, but I'll bet the public library has a directory of nursing homes in the state."

"Thanks. That's a great idea," I said. "I know just what I'll send her first."

Saturday, October 9

I helped Dad take down the screens and
put up the storm windows. We sat on the back
steps eating apples. Looking across the yard,
we could see Mrs. Wheeler putting something in
her toolshed.

"Hi, Mrs. Wheeler," I shouted.

She turned toward us and waved. Dad and
I waved back. Down the street, a door slammed.
We saw Trotter stomp into his backyard holding
a rake.

"Looks like he has joined the work force,"
Dad observed.

We watched as Trotter looked around the
backyard, then sat down on his back steps.
He kept trying to balance the rake upside-
down on the palm of his hand. Each time, it
clattered to the ground. On his last attempt,

the rake banged into the side of the house,
narrowly missing the kitchen window.

Trotter's mother came to the back door and
pointed a finger at him.

"If you break a window, you're in deep
trouble, mister," she yelled. "Start raking the
yard right this minute!"

Trotter scowled and began to rake.

We chuckled. I had told Dad about Trotter's
schemes to get out of doing chores. Then Dad
glanced over at Trotter and said soberly, "This
may sound crazy, but I feel sorry for him."

What's even crazier is that I felt sorry for
him, too.

Tuesday, October 12
<< 3:29 P.M. >>

Mitch: Hi, Wootie. Did you get my package?

MapleG: I certainly did. I loved your note, but I especially love the maple leaf. I keep it in the drawer of my bedside table. I look at it every night before I go to sleep. It's such a beautiful shade of red. Is it from your yard?

Mitch: No. I found it on the sidewalk when I was walking home from school one day. We learned how to preserve them in art class. You just put one between two sheets of wax paper and iron them. The wax melts and coats the leaf. Now you're not Maple-less anymore.

MapleG: That's right. Thank you, Mitchell.

Mitch: Any news on moving to Sherbrooke?

MapleG: As a matter of fact, Patrick and Lisa were here on Sunday. They were cleaning out my house. It looks like we have a buyer for it. I'm near the top of the waiting list for the Sherbrooke Residence Apartments. I should have a spot there within the month, they said.

Mitch: That's great.

MapleG: I know I've complained about this place a lot, but there are some things I'll miss.

Mitch: Like what?

MapleG: Like Wallace. And I've become pretty good friends with Fran, too. And of course, my O.L.D. Friend.

Mitch: That reminds me, Wootie. I was telling my dad about your move to Sherbrooke. He said it's only about an hour and a half from here. He said he'd be glad to drive me over for a visit.

MapleG: I'd love that. Maybe I can really give you that hug someday. I could teach you how to play pinochle, too.

Mitch: That would be great. I'll bring the prizes.

MapleG: You'd better bring some of those cards with the big numbers, too. My old eyes don't see as well as they once did.

Mitch: It's a deal. Wootie, Officer Mac said that I have to be done early today. He has to fill out some forms releasing me from the program. I have to be going pretty soon. Will you send me your new address when you move?

MapleG: Of course I will. I saved your address off the corner of your package. Thanks again for the maple leaf.

Mitch: Sure. Bye, Wootie.

MapleG: Bye, Mitchell.

< JAN SIEBOLD >

< < 3:50 P. M. > >

I walked out of the room. Officer Mac was sitting at a desk filling out a form. He told me that he'd meet me in the parking lot in a few minutes.

I went outside and stood by the patrol car. A green and gold maple leaf was trapped under the windshield wiper. I pulled it out and tossed it in the air. The wind caught the leaf and swirled it away.

Just then Officer Mac came across the parking lot.

"Well, Mitchell," he said. "This is it. Let's get you home."

"Okay. I'm ready," I said.

I thought of that day in September when I had walked into the police station for my first chat with Wootie. Neither one of us had been ready to face the truth back then. I guess we both needed an old friend to help us figure things out.

Now it was time to move on.

< < About the Author > >

Jan Siebold lives in East Aurora, New York, where she is a school librarian. Her first novel, *Rope Burn*, was selected for the master reading lists of the Texas Bluebonnet Award and New Mexico's Land of Enchantment Book Award.

Jan and her husband, Jim, enjoy hiking, biking, and traveling. She also likes "doing time" with a good book.